How do you feel?

Written by Gillian Liu
Illustrated by Jane Green

Evans

Evans Brothers Limited

KT-153-735

shy   happy   cross   proud   scared

What a busy week! On Monday
I started my new school.

brave   sad   lonely   excited   sleepy

I felt so shy I hid behind daddy's leg!

shy   happy   cross   proud   scared

On Tuesday I met my new friend
Sam and we read lots of books.

I felt so happy I smiled and smiled.

shy　　happy　　cross　　proud　　scared

On Wednesday I made a model,
but my little sister broke it.

brave   sad   lonely   excited   sleepy

I felt so cross I stamped my feet.

shy   happy   cross   proud   scared

On Thursday I helped my sister
build a model of her own.

I felt so proud I stood up tall.

shy   happy   cross   proud   scared

On Friday I went to the dentist.
I held daddy's hand.

I felt so scared my legs were shaking.

shy   happy   cross   proud   scared

The dentist was very kind.
I opened my mouth wide.

I felt very brave.
I grinned and grinned.

shy   happy   cross   proud   scared

On Saturday I lost my teddy.
I felt so sad.

brave   sad   lonely   excited   sleepy

In bed that night I felt so lonely without my teddy.

shy   happy   cross   proud   scared

Today is Sunday. It's my birthday and .... Look what I have found!

I feel so excited
I want to jump up and down.

brave sad lonely excited sleepy

Now I feel so sleepy.
It's been a very busy week.

Activities

Face puppets

You will need
2 paper plates
1 lollipop stick
felt tip pens
or crayons
wool
glue

1. Put the lollipop stick between the two plates.

2. Stick the two plates together.

3. Draw on the faces — happy on one side, sad on the other side.

4. Stick on wool for the hair.

What other faces can you draw on your plates?

Now you can try to make face puppets using paper bags.

cross

surprised

Weather chart

Look at the weather every day for a week and make your own weather chart.

March	Sunday	Monday	Tuesday
	rainy	cloudy	sunny
Wednesday	Thursday	Friday	Saturday
windy	snowy	foggy	icy

Now look at your weather chart.

Which day was rainy?

When was it cloudy?

Which day was sunny?

Which day was windy?

Today it is _____.

Yesterday it was _____.

Tomorrow it will be _____.